THE LEGEND OF HOBART

HEATHER MULLALY

FAVORED OAK PRESS

ISBN: 978-1-7364773-8-0

Book Cover Design & Formatting
by JD&J Design

For
Allison the Courageous

TABLE OF CONTENTS

CHAPTER 1
In Which I Set Out on a Quest 7

CHAPTER 2
In Which I Receive Four Magical Gifts....................13

CHAPTER 3
In Which I Meet a Very Nasty Wolf......................21

CHAPTER 4
In Which I Accidentally Drown Tate 30

CHAPTER 5
In Which I Have My First Duel 39

CHAPTER 6
In Which the Almanac Finally Proves Useful 46

CHAPTER 7
In Which Albert Walks on Water 53

CHAPTER 8
In Which We Are Set Upon by Bandits 60

CHAPTER 9
In Which We Reach the Castle...........................68

CHAPTER 10
In Which I Come Nose-to-Nose with a Dragon 74

CHAPTER 11
In Which I Travel Home Again..........................82

Acknowledgements 92

CHAPTER 1
In Which I Set Out on a Quest

In case you're wondering, becoming a hero is not as easy as you might think.

I tried rescuing a damsel in distress. But all of our local damsels practice martial arts and assured me that the last thing they needed was rescuing.

Saving a baby from a fire would have been perfect, but the housewives in Finnagen are far too careful. We haven't had a decent kitchen fire in years.

Last spring, when a bull broke out of its pasture, I thought I had found my chance. But when I caught up with the bull, the stupid animal managed to hook his horns through my belt and flip me up onto his head. William the Tormentor already called me *Ho-brat* instead of Hobart. After that day, he started calling me *Ho-brat Bull Hat.*

To not be called *Ho-brat* for the rest of my life, I needed to become a knight. To get into the King's School for the Education of Future Knights, I had to become a hero before May Day of my twelfth year. It was already early spring.

I was running out of time and ideas when I heard the news: a local maiden had been kidnapped by an ogre. Ogres don't usually come this far east. And their hides are so thick that martial arts are useless against them. This was a once-in-a-lifetime opportunity.

I didn't own any real weapons, so I took the pitchfork I used to clean out the pigpens and set out to face my first ogre.

The ogre wasn't hard to find. It had left a ten-foot-wide trail of wreckage through the forest, all the way up to the mouth of an enormous cave. I paused for a minute outside. Ogres are big and strong. But if saving damsels was easy, it wouldn't be the work of heroes.

I tightened my grip on my pitchfork and started into the cave. Halfway down the tunnel, I began to smell the smoke. The farther I went, the thicker it got. I started to cough. My eyes were watering and my nose running as I stumbled forward. Unable to see anything, I eventually tripped and fell face-first onto the ground.

There, sprawled out on my belly, I got my first good look at the cave. There was a fire up ahead of me, its flames licking wet tree branches and sending out thick smoke. The ogre lay on its side wearing nothing but a filthy loincloth. The creature's skin was covered in mud and dirt. Its head lolled to one side; its dull yellow eyes stared off at nothing in particular. Sitting at the ogre's head, happily braiding its greasy hair, was a little girl. By little, I do not mean petite. I mean young. This was no maiden on the verge of womanhood. This was a child, no older than five or six, with blonde curls, rosy cheeks, and a mouth like a bow.

The little girl looked over at me and smiled. "Hello," she said in a sweet voice. "Would you like to play too?"

"N-no," I said, peeling myself up off the floor. I tried to stand, my head came into the path of the smoke, and I started coughing again. I dropped down onto my knees, coughing so hard I thought I might hack up a lung.

The little girl tilted her head, observing me with interest. "That's what he did," she said, pointing to the dazed ogre. "But he bumped his head when he fell."

I pulled in a few haggard breaths and managed to choke out, "W-we have to g-go."

"But we were going to have a tea party."

"W-we'll do it at h-home," I said before breaking into another string of hacking coughs.

"All right," she said brightly and stood up, patting the ogre on the head before skipping over to me.

The little girl didn't cough or wheeze. Her eyes stayed perfectly clear and her nose dry—because she was so short that she walked *under* the smoke. There are times when life is remarkably unfair.

The child smiled when she reached me and held out one dimpled hand. I accepted her small hand, and half crouching, I started us back toward the mouth of the cave.

Even that low, I still breathed in too much smoke, and I couldn't see anything. I told myself it didn't matter how miserable I was or how young the girl. I had still managed to save a damsel. No one had to know that she hadn't actually been in distress. I would be a hero, and certainly her family would be willing to speak for me. I was sure I had finally done it.

Until we made it out of the cave.

There, in front of us, stood a line of horsemen. The Lord of Finnagen was mounted in the center, his nephew, William the Tormentor, on the horse to his right. The men all stared at me, half crouched, eyes watering, nose running, being led out of the cave by a small child.

William let out an enormous laugh. "*Ho-brat* got saved by a little girl!"

"Th-that's not wh-what happened," I stammered.

"He's coming to my tea party," the little girl said with a broad smile.

The laughter just got louder.

"Do you need a hairbow for your tea party, *Ho-brat?*" William said between snorts of laughter.

Usually, William pegged me with tomatoes. But we were far enough out of the village that there were no tomatoes at hand. So William kicked his horse into motion and started bearing down on me. I scampered to the side, slipped, and fell headlong into the mud.

The laughter was deafening.

The little girl started toward me; her small hand

stretched out to help me up. But I pulled away and ran toward home. The laughter trailed after me.

Maybe, my life would have been different if I hadn't started stuttering when I was five. Or if my mother hadn't given me the name Hobart. She named my older brothers after heroes. She named me after a jester she saw at a fair. The man got laughed at for a living. But she thought his name would be a good choice for her son.

I didn't want to see anyone. And when I reached my family's pig farm, I thought about hiding in the barn. But hunger won out, and I went into the house. My family was finishing up supper. They all looked up and saw me with my coating of mud.

"What did you do, wrestle a pig?" my brother George said.

"If he did, he lost," Michael said.

They all laughed.

Our father just said, "You're late. Supper is over."

"Y-yes, sir," I mumbled and ducked out of the room before Mother could fuss at me about the mud.

When I walked into the kitchen, our cook, Maude, looked up from the bread she was kneading. She sighed.

"What happened?"

I told her everything.

She had to fight back a smile at times, but Maude is a good woman. She didn't laugh. She set out food for me and started heating water for a bath.

Sopping up stew with my bread, I began to think. The memories of the day tried to bully their way in, but I pushed them away. Remembering my humiliation was not going to help. I needed a plan.

By the time I finished my stew, I was sure. If I still wanted to make it into knight school after this latest debacle, there was only one possibility left. I was going to have to slay a dragon.

It was risky, I know. But I saw no other choice. I was desperate. (When minstrels tell their tales, they always seem to dwell on heroes' sense of duty. They completely overlook the equally powerful driving force called *desperation*.)

I took my bath and went to bed. When my brothers came into the loft, I pretended to be asleep, but I was actually thinking and planning. At least as much as you can really plan an epic adventure.

The very next morning, I set out. I had no horse, no sword or shield. The only things I carried were my eating knife and a small sack of food that Maude had packed for me.

"Safe journey, child," she said as she handed me the satchel.

My parents stood in the doorway watching us.

"Have fun playing dragon slayer," my mother called after me.

She and Father smiled knowingly as I left. I'm sure they thought that I would be home by dark.

They were wrong.

CHAPTER 2
In Which I Receive Four Magical Gifts

By sundown, I was in the village of Gretten. When I reached the cottage that a townsman had pointed out as belonging to Mildred the Wise, I knocked and was invited inside. I stepped through the low doorway and dropped to one knee in front of the small woman sitting by the fire. (It never hurts to be polite to someone who could probably turn you into a toad.)

"W-wisest Mildred," I said in my most solemn voice, "I s-seek your c-counsel to find a dragon, that I may s-slay the vile beast and become w-worthy of entering the K-King's S-School for the E-Education of Future Knights."

I had spent most of the day practicing that speech.

"Do you always have a stutter, or only when you're trying to speak to wise women?" Mildred asked.

"A-always."

Mildred gave me a look that seemed to see past my skin. "What is your name, young would-be knight?"

"H-Hobart Septavious of F-Finnagen."

"That is a doozy," Mildred said, "but not the worst I've ever heard."

"W-what was the w-worst?"

"Peevish Petterbottom," she said immediately.

That was admittedly worse, but since poor Peevish didn't live in Finnagen, it didn't do me much good.

"W-will you h-help me?" I really didn't know who else to ask if she said no.

Mildred tilted her head, watching me. "Perhaps," she said. "You know that to be eligible to take the examination for the King's School for the Education of Future Knights, you must be nominated by three individuals?"

"Y-yes."

"And how many nominations do you have?" Mildred said.

"N-none."

"Hmm," she said.

"I-I've t-tried," I told her.

Mildred gave me an assessing look and then said, "Go bring me some firewood."

I had been expecting a task, but something much more complicated than collecting wood. "Wh-where is it?" I asked.

Her expression turned sharp.

"I'll f-find it," I said and started out through the front door.

I found the neat little woodpile on the back side of the cottage, collected an armload of logs, and went back inside. Mildred promptly set me to work building a fire, peeling carrots, and then setting the table. Soon we sat down to supper.

Mildred turned out to be a fine cook, and I enjoyed the food, if not the conversation. From a long string of questions, she learned almost everything I wanted to keep to myself. That I was the seventh son of a pig farmer. That I had been stuttering since I was five. And that I was tormented by William, the nephew of our local lord.

"So you think that becoming a knight will solve all of your problems?" Mildred said.

"P-people don't t-taunt men with s-swords," I told her.

"It helps if the men actually know how to use the swords," Mildred said.

"W-which is why I want to go to s-school."

"Not to serve the king and protect his people?" Mildred said.

"Th-that too."

Mildred raised an eyebrow at me but didn't comment.

When our bowls were empty, Mildred folded her small hands. "Are you set on a dragon?"

"Y-yes," I told her. "I've t-tried everything else."

"Dragons are highly unpredictable."

"I kn-know."

"And have large appetites," Mildred said, watching me with a critical eye.

I nodded. It was easier.

"Well, there is only one dragon left in this part of the world. He lives at Castle Flamegon in southern Rona. But there is no use in leaving for Rona until the morning. You can stay here tonight."

"Th-thank you." I was glad to spend at least one more night under a roof. I didn't really know where I would sleep after that. Along the road, I guessed.

When the dishes had been cleared, I wrapped myself up in my cloak, lay down by the fire, and went to sleep.

That night, I dreamt that I was standing in a massive hall with a sword gripped in my right hand. The ceiling was distant, the floor covered in flattened gold coins. Lit torches sat in brackets along the walls. On the far side of the room was an enormous heap of treasure: gold and jewels, weapons, and crowns. And lying on top of the mound was a dragon. The beast was larger than I had thought possible. His green scales shimmered in the torchlight. His wings were folded, his eyes shut. Even with his mouth closed, I could see his teeth—white and sharp and as long as my forearm.

Why had I decided to try and kill this monster? I couldn't remember exactly. But then figures appeared along the edges of the room. I knew their faces even before William started the chant, "*Ho-brat,* bull hat!"

My chin came up and my hand tightened around the sword's hilt as the first tomato left William's hand. I started down the hall, trying to ignore my uninvited audience.

Which wasn't easy, between the chanting and the flying fruit.

I used my left hand to wipe the mess out of my eyes and kept walking. But then the laughter reached new heights. I looked down to see that my clothes were gone, along with my sword. I stood completely naked, covered in tomato, holding nothing but a stick. The laughter echoed through the hall, building into a deafening noise.

Until the dragon opened his eyes.

I froze. The crowd drew back, suddenly silent as the dragon stared at me with silver eyes. Then the beast began to climb down from his pile of treasure.

"You come to best me with a stick?" The creature's voice was low and rough like thunder.

"I h-had a s-sword," I said.

"You seem to have misplaced it," the dragon said.

And then he ate me.

I woke up covered in what I thought was dragon drool. It took me a minute to realize that it was sweat, and then another minute to remember where I was. Mildred the Wise slept nearby; her hands tucked beneath her head. She chuckled in her sleep, rolled over, and began to snore. I did my best to go back to sleep, but my thoughts kept chasing after my dream. I couldn't help but wonder what it would feel like to be eaten.

The next morning, Mildred and I broke our fast on porridge, and then I got ready to start out on my journey. Before I left, Mildred said that she would like to present me with gifts. I felt a surge of relief. Not only was this wise woman going to give me a much-needed sword, but it might even be a legendary blade. Even I would have a chance of slaying a dragon if I had a legendary blade.

"First, take this," Mildred said, and with great ceremony, handed me a large book. I tried to cover my disappointment, but apparently failed. Because she snapped, "What's wrong with it?"

"N-Nothing," I said. "I was just h-hoping for a s-sword."

"A sword, heavens!" Mildred said. "If you had a sword, you would probably poke out your eye. No, this book will be much more useful. It's an almanac. It's not perfect at predicting the weather, but it's useful nonetheless."

I opened the book and flipped through the pages until I found the current date. "It s-says that it w-will be s-sunny today," I said, and then looked from the window, which showed a steady drizzle, back to Mildred.

"I told you it wasn't perfect," she said. "Your second gift is this magical satchel. No matter how many times you empty it, it will always fill again."

Now this sounded more promising. "Wh-what does it h-hold?"

"Turnips," Mildred said, clearly pleased.

"T-turnips?" What was I supposed to do with an endless supply of turnips?

"They can be used in all sorts of delicious dishes," Mildred said. "Fried turnips, sautéed turnips, baked turnips, turnip soup, turnip stew, turnip kabobs. . ."

"I g-get the idea," I told her, but then I had to ask, "Wh-what's the difference between turnip s-soup and turnip st-stew?"

"Potatoes. Now, your third gift is this spool of unbreakable thread. The only thing that can cut it is a diamond."

"D-do you have a d-diamond?" I asked.

"No, I don't like the look of them," Mildred said.

I was beginning to think that stopping at Mildred's had been a complete waste of time.

"I have one last gift to aid you on your journey," Mildred said with great ceremony.

"I-I thought it was t-traditional to give a h-hero three g-gifts," I said.

Mildred shrugged. "I'm a nonconformist, and you are no hero. Not yet anyway. You have quite a few things to learn first."

"L-like what?" I asked, hoping for any clues this riddle of a wise woman might give me about how to slay a dragon.

"You will learn them when the time comes," Mildred said. "But first, follow me."

I was not interested in hauling any more useless stuff, but Mildred gave me a look, and I followed. We walked through the light rain to a small building behind the cottage. Inside stood a fine white horse. My spirits immediately rose. I no longer cared that Mildred had given me an almanac that didn't predict the weather and an endless supply of turnips. This noble creature would make up for it all.

But then I had a terrible thought. What if she planned to give me a tired old donkey instead? I looked around, but the horse was the only creature in sight.

"Hobart, I would like to introduce you to Albert. Albert, this is your new master, Hobart. You will be accompanying him on his quest."

"A quest, how exciting."

I looked up at the horse, confused.

"I do hope that you are planning to wait until after the rain stops, though. I hate getting my hooves wet." The horse looked at me with a worried expression. "Goodness knows we wouldn't want me to catch cold."

"Don't be such a baby, Albert," Mildred said to the horse. "A little damp won't hurt you."

I just stared at the two of them as I realized that this strange little sage was offering to give me a talking horse. I couldn't decide if that was a good thing or a bad thing.

By the end of the day, I was sure. It was a bad thing.

CHAPTER 3
In Which I Meet a Very Nasty Wolf

Albert spent our first morning together telling me his life story, from his first days as a foal through his career as a member of the king's cavalry and right up to the day he was given to Mildred the Wise as a gift of thanks. I guessed that his former owner had more likely given Albert away in a desperate attempt to find silence, but I kept that opinion to myself.

The afternoon brought me a litany of details about Albert's likes (he was extremely fond of chocolate), his dislikes (anything messy or muddy), his fears (which went on for close to an hour and seemed to revolve around blood, disease, and spiders), and his dreams (including one day seeing a statue of himself in the center of the main square of King's City).

The sun was beginning to set as we traveled along the road to Jolip. I was busy daydreaming about trading Albert in for a nice mute pony when the horse suddenly started to shake.

"Oh, my goodness," Albert cried.

His front hooves came up off the ground, and I could see one of his eyes rolling around in terror. Albert shrieked as his hooves struck the road again, and then he began to gallop. I threw myself onto his neck, grabbing fistfuls of mane just to hang on.

I yelled at Albert to stop. He yelled back at me, though I couldn't make out a word. I thought he had completely lost his mind. Until I saw what had turned my horse into a maniac. Up ahead of us, a pile of clothes lay in the middle of the road. Crouched beside the clothes was a massive gray wolf. The beast was watching Albert with bright yellow eyes.

Suddenly, I was yelling at Albert to *go*, but he couldn't seem to manage a straight line to save either of our lives. The horse ran in jagged circles, screaming. I clung to his neck, trying not to get thrown off and trampled—or worse, eaten. The wolf watched us, then eased to his shaggy feet, his eyes never leaving the horse. The light was dim, but I could still see the animal's teeth. I was waiting for him to pounce. But instead, with wary glances at the screaming horse, the wolf slunk back into the woods.

It took me several minutes to convince Albert that the wolf was gone, and he could stop galloping in spastic circles. Finally, Albert stopped. His coat was covered with sweat and his sides were heaving. I climbed shakily down from the saddle. Once I was off his back, Albert lay down and put his nose between his front hooves. He took deep, labored breaths. I leaned against a tree.

From where I stood, I could see the lump of clothes still lying in the middle of the road. The longer I looked at them, the less empty they seemed. With a sick feeling in my stomach, I pushed off from the tree trunk and walked slowly toward the pile. My hands were cold, and my legs could not seem to work right, but my thoughts were clear. *Please don't be dead.* I had no idea what to do with a dead body, let alone what the sight of one would do to my horse.

To my great relief, the clothes began to move. Slowly, a head appeared, followed by long, skinny limbs. The shape of a tall boy unfolded. Beneath him I saw a small lamb. The boy turned around and looked at me.

"You—you saved us from the wolf," the boy said.

I honestly had no idea what to say to this. And then, as if this day hadn't been strange enough already, he knelt, in the mud, in front of me.

"I am in your debt, sir," he said.

My face grew suddenly hot, and my jaw tightened until it hurt. I had been mocked my entire life. I didn't need to take this from a stranger. I turned around and walked over to where Albert was still lying on the ground.

"G-get up," I told him.

Albert moaned.

"You're not h-hurt. G-get up." I had no patience left for this horse.

The boy approached me carefully.

"Did I offend you, sir?" he asked.

"N-no," I snapped. "And s-stop calling me 's-sir.'"

"Should I call you 'my lord'?"

"N-no." What was wrong with him?

The boy shifted his weight back and forth between his feet. "I don't know what to do, then," he said.

"Take your lamb and go h-home," I told him and then grabbed hold of Albert's reins and pulled.

"I am having heart palpitations," Albert moaned.

"N-no, you're n-not," I said.

The boy was staring at my horse, who had rolled onto his side moaning. "He talked," the boy said.

"H-he does that," I said, with a look of great annoyance at my horse.

The boy shook his head as if to clear the cobwebs out of his thoughts. "I can't," he told me.

"You c-can't what?"

"I can't go home," the boy said, "at least, not unless you come with me. You saved my life. I'm in your debt until I do the same for you."

"I-I did not s-save your life," I nearly shouted.

"But you did," the boy said, nodding vigorously. "If you and your noble steed hadn't come along, the wolf would have killed me and Dolly."

Albert's ears perked up at the words "noble steed."

"Look," I said slowly. "I'm g-glad that you didn't g-get e-eaten, but I didn't mean to s-save you. I d-didn't even re-alize that you were a p-person until after the w-wolf left."

The boy shook his head firmly. "It doesn't matter how it happened. I have to stay with you until I repay my debt."

I just stared at him.

"Come home with me for supper," he said.

He seemed serious, and I was more than a little hungry.

"My family will want to meet you," the boy said. "And my mother is an excellent cook. She would be happy to have you."

I finally gave in.

The boy beamed at me. "I am Tate of Fair Oaks."

"H-hobart of F-Finnagen," I said, and then waited for the comments and the laughter.

"Good to meet you, Hobart," Tate said cheerfully.

"G-good to m-meet you too," I said, more than a little surprised.

We talked Albert back up onto his hooves and then climbed onto his back. Tate used one arm to hold on to me and the other to hold on to Dolly the lamb. I hoped that Albert would behave himself.

"Wh-which w-way?" I asked Tate.

"Straight ahead," he told me.

So Albert started out, still shaking on occasion and moaning quietly to himself, but he didn't buck or gallop. Tate took over the talking.

"You'll like Fair Oaks," he said. "It's a real friendly village. My family has lived there for ten generations. My great-great-grandfather kept the sheep of Lord Dillingham himself. When his lordship died, he left my great-great-grandfather a flock of his own. My family have been independent shepherds ever since."

We came over a small rise, and Tate straightened up. "There's Fair Oaks," he said. "My house is the first on the right."

Tate pointed out a large, well-kept cottage. The wooden shutters stood open, letting warm firelight and the comfortable smell of freshly baked bread seep out into the evening air.

As Albert stopped in front of the house, the door opened. A cluster of blonde children spilled out into the yard, followed by a round blonde woman.

Tate slid awkwardly down off Albert's back, set Dolly on her own small hooves, and then was instantly mobbed by the throng of people. His little brothers and sisters pulled on him. His mother hugged him and then led him into the house. I hung back, standing as close to Albert as I could, until Tate's mother looked back over her shoulder at me.

"Come along, dear," she said. "Terrance will look after your horse."

A boy of about ten took Albert's reins from me, and then a small hand grasped mine. I looked down at a little girl.

"Come on, Tate's friend," she said with a smile. "Mama has supper ready."

Tate's little sister led me into the cottage. It was as warm and cozy on the inside as it looked from the outside.

A stone hearth covered one entire wall. A large bed stood on the opposite wall. Above the bed was a sleeping loft that housed a line of beds, each covered with a patchwork quilt. In the middle of the room was one long wooden table.

In the firelight, I got my first good look at Tate. He was tall and skinny, with golden hair that stood out from his head like straw. He had a round face and bright blue eyes above a broad smile. It was a face I saw scattered throughout the room in various sizes. I counted eight children, five boys and three girls. A large man with the same twinkling eyes came over to introduce himself and shake my hand. The round woman settled me on a bench at the table. The places on either side of me quickly filled with small, eager faces.

At first, there was a jumble of chatter as bowls of stew and chunks of bread were passed. But then Tate began to tell the story of his encounter with the wolf. All other conversation stopped as every face turned toward him in expectation.

"I had just found Dolly when the sun started to set," Tate said. "We made it as far as the last hill before home, and then something moved off in the woods." He paused, looking around the table. "It came closer, and I saw that it was a wolf!"

A few of the smaller children gasped.

"It came toward us, slow and growling," he said. "I reached back for my staff, but it was gone."

"No," a little boy whispered.

"I threw a few rocks at the beast, but it just kept coming, its eyes glowing yellow." Tate was clearly enjoying himself. "Dolly tried to run. The wolf leapt in her direction. And I did the only thing I could. I threw my body over hers and waited to die."

One little sister clapped her hand over her mouth.

"But then I heard hoofbeats pounding down the road, and a great white horse burst onto the scene. Brave Hobart of Finnagen had arrived!" Tate said. "He charged the wolf, circling around us, and drove off the beast, sending it slinking back into the woods with its tail tucked between its legs!"

The table erupted into applause. A brother reached over to clap me on the back. Tate's mother came over to hug me, dabbing tears from her eyes.

"You saved my boy," she cried, and then hugged me again.

"I j-just h-happened to be there at the right t-time," I said weakly.

"And he's modest, no less," Tate's father announced. He reached across the table to shake my hand. "You are welcome at our table anytime. What a lad!"

"And he has a talking horse," Tate said.

That statement caused an uproar.

"How did you get a talking horse?" one little boy asked with wide eyes.

"M-Mildred the W-Wise gave him to me, to h-help me on my journey," I said.

"Where are you going?" an older boy asked.

"T-to Rona, to try and k-kill a dr-dragon," I said, feeling awkward.

"A quest!" Tate's father said. "The boy ventures out on a quest, and our Tate is to accompany him! What a day!"

No one could seem to talk about anything else for the rest of the meal. They peppered me with questions. Tate's family wanted to know all about me and my travels so far. They were awed by Mildred's gifts, and when supper was finished, we all had to travel out to the shed to speak to Albert, who thoroughly enjoyed the attention.

That night, I lay in the sleeping loft under a patchwork quilt, warm and well fed, surrounded by the soft snores of Tate and his siblings. But I couldn't sleep. This whole household of people thought I was a hero headed out on a noble quest. What would they think of me if I failed? With a tightness in my stomach, I realized that coming back to Fair Oaks in disgrace would be even worse than being *Ho-brat* of Finnagen for the rest of my life.

CHAPTER 4
In Which I Accidentally Drown Tate

The next morning, Tate, Albert, and I left Fair Oaks. All of Tate's family, and most of the village, came out to send us off. The women embraced us. The girls kissed our cheeks. Boys shook our hands. Men gave us last bits of advice:

"Keep your eyes open."

"Don't trust any man dressed in silk."

"Look after your horse. You don't want to have to walk home."

Not a single person in the whole village laughed or said that we would be home by dinner. Most of them probably figured that they would never see us again, but at least they had the good manners not to say so.

Albert was glowing, and not just because Tate's brothers had given him a good brushing. The horse had an audience, and he was enjoying every minute of it. He pranced his way down the main street of Fair Oaks, tossing his head to make his bridle jingle. I finally gave up on the reins, since he was clearly going to do what he wanted.

Tate rode behind me again. He held on with one arm and waved to his village with the other.

"I'll bring back dragon gold!" he yelled.

I wasn't sure that was the wisest promise, but the crowd cheered. Small children ran along beside us, waving.

Tate's mother had to yell to be heard over the noise. "Take care of each other."

"Such brave boys," an elderly woman said as we passed her.

We reached the edge of the small village, and I glanced back once, just to see the waving crowd, before the road turned to the left and Fair Oaks disappeared from sight.

Tate talked almost constantly that first morning, all about the adventures we were going to have and the stories he would get to carry home. But I didn't hear much of what he said. That old woman's words kept bouncing around inside my mind, and I had to wonder: *Am I really brave?* I had tried more than a few foolish things in my attempts to become a hero; but I wasn't sure that any of them counted as acts of bravery. I wasn't sure that I even knew what brave really meant.

When the sun reached the center of the sky, we stopped to eat and then rode all afternoon. By nightfall, we were so tired that we just ate some of the food Tate's mother had sent, lay down beside a small stream, and went to sleep. The next morning, I was stiff and sore. Tate laughed as I hobbled around like an old man.

"I'm guessing you haven't slept on the ground much," he said.

"N-no," I said.

"You'll get used to it."

I highly doubted that.

No one had told me that becoming a hero was so uncomfortable or frustrating. That night we tried to build a fire. Since neither of us had a flint, we tried the "spinning stick" method. If anyone ever tries to tell you that this means of starting a fire is easy, know that person is a liar.

The way it works is you make a little notch in one stick; then you stand another stick up in the notch. You spin the standing stick back and forth between your hands until you develop blisters, begin thinking dark thoughts about the inventor of the spinning stick method, or actually create a spark. Tate got blisters. I thought dark thoughts. We never did make fire.

After two days of riding, spending hours attempting to make sparks, and falling onto the ground exhausted each night, we ran out of the food Tate's mother had given us. So we turned to the magic turnip satchel. I half expected the thing to stay empty, considering our recent luck, but it filled itself up, just as Mildred had promised. We didn't have any spices or even a way to cook the things, but when you're hungry enough, anything tastes good, for a while.

On our third day past Fair Oaks, we came to a river. On the opposite side, I could make out a faint continuation of our road, but there was also a track worn into the dirt that turned to the north, avoiding the water. We had crossed a few creeks, but this river was wide, and the waters were moving swiftly. Spanning the river was a rickety-looking bridge. A sign in front of the bridge read:

It is hereby decreed that this bridge is from now on and forevermore closed to all traffic, by order of the Lord of Greenville.

Good sense would have suggested that we turn north and follow the path made by hundreds of feet. But I was tired and hungry and admittedly grumpy. And all I really wanted to do was get to Rona and either kill a dragon or be eaten by one and be done with this whole miserable trip. I turned Albert toward the bridge.

"That structure does not look sound," Albert said.

"I-It's fine," I told him.

"I will most likely slip and sprain a hoof or tumble into the river to my death," he moaned.

"N-No one is g-going to die."

"Are you sure it's safe?" This was Tate now. He had at least proven to not be a complainer, but he did sound concerned, and, looking back, I had to admit he had good reason. The bridge seemed to sag, and the wood looked old and brittle.

But I wasn't in a mood to be reasonable. "The b-bridge is fine. We're g-going over it."

Tate and Albert exchanged glances, but neither said anything more, and we started forward.

Albert moaned a little as the bridge groaned under the weight of his front hooves, but when nothing happened, he gingerly continued across. The structure made a symphony of creaks and small snapping noises, but it held stable until we reached the middle of the river. When we had come to nearly the exact center of the bridge, the wood started to move.

"G-get down," I told Tate and then swung down off Albert's back.

I thought that if we spread out our weight, things might go better. But as soon as our shoes touched the wooden planks, the entire structure collapsed.

We fell through the air, surrounded by boards broken into jagged shapes, and then plunged into the river. It felt like I fell forever. But finally, my feet touched the bottom. I pushed off, pulling with my arms and kicking with my feet, trying to reach the sunlight. The light seemed to keep moving farther and farther away, but finally my head broke through the surface.

I spent half a minute doing nothing but gasping for air. My lungs couldn't seem to get enough. But then my mind started working again. My feet kicked out, turning me in a sharp half circle as I searched the water. I saw Albert lying on the opposite bank, his large side heaving. I could faintly hear him moaning. He was fine. But where was Tate? I spun all the way around, but there was no shock of yellow hair.

I yelled his name. No one answered. The water was carrying me downstream, and I still saw no sign of Tate.

I dove down, searching for any glimpse of him, but there was nothing. I had to go up for air. With my lungs full again, I started swimming, trying to climb back up the river, closer to where we fell in. The waters fought me, but I was desperate. I struggled back up the river, ducking my head as often as I could to look for any sign of him. I knew a person couldn't survive underwater for more than a few minutes.

We were almost out of time when I saw a limp shape just under the surface. I took off. I had always been a good swimmer. It's a skill you develop when you are likely to be thrown into any body of water you pass. But that day I swam faster than I ever had in my life. When I reached Tate, I took one last huge breath of air and dove.

Tate's head was slumped forward, his eyes closed. I grabbed hold of his arms and pulled, but he didn't come up with me. I pulled harder, but he was tethered, his foot trapped in a cluster of rocks. I dove down, tugging at stones and throwing them aside until Tate came loose. Immediately he started floating down the river with the current. I grabbed him, my lungs screaming, and strained to pull us both toward the surface.

Finally, we broke through. The current carried us along as I struggled to keep Tate's unconscious head out of the water. I didn't know how I was going to get us to shore. But then a hand grabbed me and started to pull. I dragged Tate along. More hands caught hold of us and hauled us up out of the water. Soon I was gasping in the bottom of a fishing boat under the watchful eyes of two strangers.

One of the men started rowing us back toward shore. The other was busy pressing on Tate's chest. A few good pushes and Tate was turning, waves of water flowing out of his mouth, before he started to cough. By the time we reached the bank, Tate's eyes were open. I laughed. I had never been so glad to see anything in my entire life.

When I was finally convinced that he was going to live, I left Tate sitting on the riverbank with the fishermen and walked upstream to retrieve my horse. Albert was in the mood for theatrics, and for once, I didn't mind. I was so relieved to know Tate was breathing that I didn't say a word as Albert told me all about his life flashing in front of his eyes.

When Albert had finished, we walked back down to Tate and the boatmen.

"You saved my life again," Tate said when Albert and I reached him.

I felt suddenly very uncomfortable in my sopping wet clothes. "I-I also almost g-got you drowned in the f-first place," I told the dirt.

"But Dan said that you kept diving back under, looking for me. He said that you could have died trying to save me."

I shrugged, not really sure what to say about that.

"We're glad you boys are all right," one of the men said. I didn't know if he was Dan or not. "And maybe now Lord Fancy Pants will finally replace that old bridge."

His friend scoffed. "You know he won't spend a coin on anything that doesn't go into his own stomach."

Tate looked over at me. "We could build them a new bridge."

"H-how?"

"With the unbreakable thread," he said. His eyes were bright, the way they always were when he mentioned anything magical.

I started to say, "No," but he looked at me with that eager face, and I knew that I owed him this much. I nodded. Tate beamed.

We spent most of the day building a bridge. The two fishermen, who it turned out were both named Dan, ferried us back and forth across the river while we unwound the unbreakable thread, securing it on the stone posts that were the only part of the old bridge still standing. We wove thread back and forth between those first lines and then set the boards, securing each one with more thread. We even made handrails before finally burying the spool, which still seemed full.

Albert refused to try the new bridge, but Dan the Stout brought his own horse, which was thankfully silent, and walked across the bridge without incident. The whole village came out to thank us and shake our hands, and perhaps best of all, they fed us. They offered us a place to stay, but I was eager to keep going. So Tate and I climbed onto Albert's back and continued on our way.

Dan the Slight had given us a flint in thanks for the unbreakable thread, so we actually had a fire that night. We ate the food the villagers had given us and sat around the fire telling stories and laughing.

For the first time I could remember, I went to bed happy.

I woke up with a sword pointed at my face.

CHAPTER 5
In Which I Have My First Duel

In case you have never had the experience of waking up to find a weapon pointed at your face, let me walk you through it. In phase one, you are certain that you're having a nightmare. You look around, hoping to see something bizarre to confirm this. When you can't find anything else out of the ordinary, you try the classic "pinch yourself" method. Supposedly, you can't feel pain in a dream. So you pinch yourself hard enough to leave a bruise and then mumble some choice words because that not only hurt, but it means you're awake.

In phase two, you come to accept that there really is a man standing over you pointing a weapon at your face, and your body finally reacts. Your heart rate surges, you begin to sweat, and you start scuttling backward, wondering how your mortal enemy has tracked you down.

In my case, there were two problems with phase two. First, I ran into a rock. Second, I didn't have any mortal enemies, at least not that I knew of. William didn't count. If I was dead, he couldn't torment me. I guess the dragon was technically my mortal enemy, since I was on my way to try and kill it, but this man was clearly not a dragon. I had to wonder if the dragon had some sort of arrangement with the local thugs. He agrees not to eat their daughters if they kill off any knights headed for his lair.

But this man didn't look like a thug. For one thing, he was old, with gray hair and a wrinkled face. And there was something stately about him, as if he had once been a proud man. His clothes were well-made, and his beard neatly trimmed. He looked like a wild-eyed gentleman.

"Stand up and fight me, coward!" my non-thug opponent yelled. His voice and expression belonged to a man who had been seriously wronged.

I eased my way to my feet, wondering what I had done to him.

"Take up your weapon, Gordon. I will not give you a second opportunity."

Now, this made no more sense to me than it does to you. Nowhere in my string of unfortunate names was there anything even close to Gordon.

"I-I think you h-have me c-confused with s-someone else," I told him.

"Your fearful voice speaks of your weak heart," he said and then took a swing at me with the sword.

I ducked low and moved right.

My father had been very enthusiastic about teaching my brother Edward to fight. He showed similar pleasure in instructing my brother George. But by the time I reached the age of ten and my lessons should have begun, Father had long since lost interest in direct instruction. He told me that my brothers would teach me what I needed to know.

What I learned from my brothers was simple. Do not stay in one place when someone is swinging a large object at your head, and don't be above kicking and biting if you get pinned down in the dirt. So though I knew nothing about swordsmanship and didn't have a sword to use anyway, I was not completely defenseless.

The old man swung at me. I ducked and danced. I had been hit by more than a few fists, but this was a sword. The sunlight seemed to make a point of shining on the edges, just to remind me how sharp the thing was.

My opponent was old and clearly not as strong as he had once been, but I could see glimpses of skill. This man had been a great swordsman in his day. Unfortunately, he didn't need much expertise to spear me with the sharp point of a blade.

Suddenly, a large branch hit my arm. I was about to yell when I realized that Tate was handing me a weapon. The tree limb had knobs where he had torn off branches, but it still worked something like a staff. The next time the gentle-man swung at me, I blocked the blow. The impact seemed to startle him. He stumbled back. I took a step forward. He swung at me again, not as hard this time. Again, I blocked it.

The man was still yelling at me, calling me Gordon and going on about some despicable thing he was sure I had done. I tried to tell him I wasn't Gordon. But he didn't seem to hear anything I yelled back at him. I didn't want to hurt him, but I didn't want to die either.

So the next time he lifted his sword to begin the arc of a swing, I hit him square in the chest with the end of my branch. The old man fell backward, hitting the ground hard.

I walked cautiously toward him. Tate took the chance to run over and wrestle the sword out of the man's hand. I was more concerned that his eyes were wide, and he seemed to be having trouble breathing.

I knelt down next to the old man and pulled him up to a sitting position. His chest seemed to work better that way. He took in a long, labored breath.

"Who is he?" Tate said.

"I h-have no idea."

I heard hooves striking the ground and looked up, half expecting Albert to be fleeing the scene. But my horse was only a few feet away, attempting to hide behind a boulder that was a third his size. The hoofbeats came from a large dark horse that was cantering toward us. It came to a stop, and I thought about asking Tate for the sword, but then I caught sight of the rider.

It was a girl who swung down off the horse. She looked to be about our age, with long dark hair and fierce eyes.

Her voice was sharp. "What did you do to him?"

"N-Nothing," I said, suddenly realizing how bad this must look. "H-he tried to k-kill me. I defended myself."

She glared at me as Tate nodded vigorously. "It's true," Tate said. "This old fellow came at him with a sword, yelling about Gordon."

The girl's features lost their sharp edges. "Oh. I'm sorry," she said. "My grandfather gets confused."

"Your grandfather?" Tate asked.

The girl nodded. "Sir Danton of Mortico."

Tate and I both stared at her. We knew the name. Everyone did. Sir Danton of Mortico had been the king's champion years before. Not a single person had asked for trial by combat during his time in office. He was that good.

Sitting on the ground, Sir Danton seemed to have collected himself. He turned to Tate. "My sword, lad," he said.

Tate looked at me with uncertainty.

"It's all right," the girl said. "He's calm now."

I still wasn't certain this was a wise plan, but Tate handed Sir Danton back his weapon. The knight slowly worked his way up onto his knees. He laid the sword blade across his hands and looked up at me.

"You have bested me," Sir Danton said. "I present you with the sword *Guardian*."

Was he serious? I waited, thinking that he would laugh and say that it had all been in jest. But he stayed there, holding the sword.

"I c-can't accept it," I said.

Sir Danton held the blade out to me anyway.

I turned to look at the girl, hoping that she could convince him. She was staring at me with her head tilted to the side and lines forming between her brows.

"You have a stutter," she said.

The back of my neck felt hot, and my lips closed tight. I nodded, waiting for the mocking to start, but she made no other comment about it.

"Take the sword," she said. "To not accept it would be to dishonor him."

"But *G-Guardian* is a legendary blade."

"Take the sword," she said. "Let him keep his dignity."

This still seemed wrong to me, but I accepted the sword. For a large weapon, *Guardian* felt incredibly light in my hand. The metal shimmered and glowed—as if a fire burned inside it—and a tingling feeling moved through my right hand and up my arm. I felt the sensation spreading through my body and wondered if I had just been poisoned. But I didn't feel any pain or weakness. If anything, I felt stronger, almost powerful.

I looked back at the knight in wonder. He nodded, looking pleased, and then his eyes seemed far away again.

The girl reached down and helped her grandfather slowly back to his feet. "My name is Hero," she said once his age-spotted arm was draped over her small shoulders.

On another day I might have thought it remarkably unfair that this girl had been gifted with the name *Hero* while I was stuck with Hobart, but in that particular moment, I was too filled with wonder to care.

"I am H-Hobart," I told her. "And this is T-tate." He nodded politely. "And Albert." I gestured to the white stallion, who was peeking out from behind his rock.

"Are you traveling?" Hero asked as she slowly walked her grandfather back toward the dark horse.

"Y-yes, to Rona." I put Sir Danton's other arm over my shoulders. All of his strength seemed to have disappeared.

"I would very much like for you to stay with us, then," Hero said. "Our home is on the road to Rona, and you both look as if you could use a bath and a hot meal."

It seemed wrong to take anything else from this family, but her offer was very tempting. Tate and Albert were suddenly both walking along beside me, nodding eagerly.

"We would be g-glad of your h-hospitality," I told her.

And so, we traveled to Castle Mortico.

CHAPTER 6
In Which the Almanac Finally Proves Useful

We followed Hero, Sir Danton, and their unremarkable horse through the woods to Mortico. Albert took the opportunity to give a lengthy commentary about the morning's events. I don't know how he could claim to have seen any of it, since he had been cowering behind a rock, but to hear Albert tell the story, my duel with Sir Danton had been the match of the century.

Mildred's almanac called for rain. So we traveled under a bright blue sky to Mortico. Tate and I were speechless when we saw it. Hero's home was exactly how I had imagined a castle should look. The tall stone walls were capped off with battlements. Enormous towers stretched up into the sky, complete with flags snapping in the wind. There was even a drawbridge that lowered to span the moat.

We rode over the drawbridge and into a huge open

courtyard. It was like a scene out of a minstrel's song. A smith hammered away on a blade. A stable boy was watering horses. Several girls passed, carrying baskets of eggs.

We gave our horses over to the care of a stableman—who was rather taken aback when Albert requested hay kebabs for his breakfast—and followed Hero and Sir Danton into the castle. The entrance hall was nearly as fantastic as the outside. Shields and tapestries lined the walls, with torches stuck in brackets between them. Everything was perfect—until we walked into the Great Hall.

The room was crowded with tables, every one of them filled with people. These individuals were not quietly breaking their fast. They filled the room with some of the stupidest conversations I have ever heard.

"I hate my horse. Why won't grandfather give me a new one?"

"That isn't sky blue; it's cornflower blue."

"Mother, he's looking at me again!"

"Reginald, you are the stupidest man alive."

"Pastries are so dull. Why can't we have something else?"

And on and on and on.

Tate and I followed Hero as she led Sir Danton to the high table at the front of the room.

"Are they always like this?" Tate asked.

"They're just getting started," she said. "Wait until

they have full bellies."

Hero brought her grandfather to his seat in the middle of the high table, and instantly the crowds surged forward like locusts descending on a new crop of wheat.

"Grandfather, I hate my room. Why can't I change with Philip?"

"Uncle, don't you think it best if I take over managing your finances?"

"Grandfather, my dresses are so out of fashion."

A middle-aged man sitting on Sir Danton's right shooed them all away.

The complainers sulked as they returned to their seats. "It's not fair," was muttered by more than a few. Sadly, most of them were adults.

"Who are these people?" Tate asked Hero as she led us toward a table in the back of the room.

"My family," Hero said, clearly annoyed. "They never visited when Grandfather actually expected something of them. But once his memory began to fade, they started turning up like mushrooms."

"Are your parents here?" Tate asked.

Hero's face lost its annoyance. "No, my parents are dead," she said, and gave us a look that made it clear the subject was closed.

After we had eaten, Hero found us a room. It was large and well furnished, but we had to share it with a boy named Melvin. Melvin did nothing but grumble about how unfair it was that I had a sword, and he didn't. I hid *Guardian* in the bottom of my bag after that. If this boy realized precisely which sword I carried, I was sure I would never hear the end of it.

That night, I decided that the beds were really the only nice thing about Castle Mortico. They were made with straw instead of rocks and had actual bed linens. Tate and I went to bed early, in part because we were tired, and in part just to get away from Hero's family.

I woke up before the sun and shook Tate. "I say we g-get out of h-here before the h-harpies wake up," I whispered.

Tate nodded and rolled out of bed, landing quietly on the rushes that covered the floor. Melvin mumbled something in his sleep, rolled over into the space where Tate had been, and went back to snoring.

We snuck our way through the castle, getting turned around more than once, and finally found the stables. Hero was waiting for us.

"I have decided to come with you to Rona," she said.

"We're going to slay a dragon," Tate said.

Hero gave us a sharp look and then shrugged her shoulders. "It doesn't really matter. I'm coming with you."

I already had more company than I could really use; but when I opened my mouth to explain that she fixed her dark eyes on me with a look that threatened my life if I gave her any trouble.

"F-fine," I told her.

Hero offered Tate a horse, but he was a little wary of

the big ones. He finally settled on a pony named Sparkles. There didn't seem to be anything sparkling about the pony's gloomy expression, but I couldn't really comment. I rode a horse named Albert.

So, we left Castle Mortico, Hero leading the way. It felt as if I was supposed to be the leader of this strange party. But since I had no idea where we were or how to get to our destination, I let her lead.

It turned out that Hero had opinions about more than just roads. That night, she told us that we had been doing nearly everything wrong. I would have grumbled at her, but her way of arranging pine needles did make for softer beds, and the turnips did taste better cooked. She even showed us which of the plants we passed were edible. I begrudgingly had to admit that we were more comfortable with her along.

Before turning north into the mountains, the road to Rona dipped south to trail along the coast. Mildred's almanac predicted snow, so of course we were covered in sweat. We were all glad to see the ocean and feel the breeze that blew in off the water.

As we rode along the edge of the beach, we saw a man huddled beside an overturned boat. Hero frowned and then turned her horse to ride over to him. Tate and I followed.

"Do you need help with your boat?" she asked.

"No," the man said in the most miserable-sounding voice I had ever heard.

Hero looked from the fishing nets stretched out on the

sand to the man.

"Aren't you a fisherman?" she said.

He nodded.

"Then why aren't you fishing?"

"There was a terrible storm last month," the man said, growing paler as he spoke. "I nearly drowned."

"You haven't gone back out on the water?" Hero asked with a frown.

"I know. I'm a coward," the man said, and then he began to cry.

"You are not a coward," she told him firmly.

Hero looked up at Tate and me with a glance that made it clear we were supposed to agree with her.

"I'm sure you're real brave," Tate said.

I looked from the ocean to the boat and then found myself walking back over to where Albert was carrying on a one-sided conversation with Sparkles. I opened my saddlebag, pulled out Mildred's almanac, and walked back to the little knot of people on the sand.

"H-here, t-take this." I handed the would-be fisherman the book. "It's an almanac."

Tate gave me a questioning glance.

Hero mouthed the words, "You said that it was always wrong."

"I-It doesn't w-work like other almanacs," I told the fisherman. "It s-says the opposite of the w-weather."

He just looked at me, confused.

"So if it s-says that it will be a s-sunny day, then you

know to expect a s-storm."

The fisherman still looked uncertain, but he took the book and opened it, turning to the day's date. "Snowy and cold," he read with the halting speech of someone who doesn't read much.

"See, it's s-sunny and h-hot," I said.

"It's always wrong?" He looked hopeful for the first time.

"Always."

We helped the fisherman turn over his boat and drag it down to the water. By the time we got back on our horses, he was loading his nets. Our group continued along the shore road, but Hero was watching me.

"It was kind of you to give him the book," she said as the road rose over a sand dune.

I shrugged. "It was h-heavy to c-carry," I said.

But I don't think she believed me.

If the fisherman checked the almanac that night, he would have chosen to stay home that next day. Because even as we slept under the stars, there was a storm brewing.

CHAPTER 7
In Which Albert Walks on Water

When we woke up the next morning, the sky was a dark, heavy gray. I kept glancing up, waiting for the first drops to fall and Albert's complaining to start, but nothing happened until late that afternoon. When the rain finally came, it fell hard and fast. We were wet to our skins within minutes and couldn't see our own hands in front of our faces.

"W-we might as well s-stop," I said, having to yell to be heard over the storm.

Hero and Tate nodded and pulled their silent horses over to the side of the trail. My horse moaned and complained. I couldn't hear most of what he said but could guess the basic idea.

We all huddled together under a tree, the branches giving us little cover from the downpour. The temperature was dropping, but we didn't have anything dry to put on, and there was no hope for starting a fire. Even

Tate looked miserable. Which was a first.

"Well, at least things can't get much worse," he said.

Seconds later, we heard the first rumbles of thunder.

Albert started to shake. Hero's horse, Virtue, began to move restlessly, her ears folded back flat against her head. Sparkles just stood there, looking as sullen as ever.

Hero stroked Virtue's head, trying to calm her, but the horses became more and more agitated as the thunder rolled closer. Albert swayed on his hooves.

"You are not g-going to faint," I told him, taking Albert by the nose. "It's just a s-storm. It c-can't hurt you."

And then the lightning struck. I might not have been able to make a fire in that rain; but the lightning managed it without any difficulty. The tree above us burst into flames, and the world exploded into chaos. The horses screamed and bucked, breaking the branch that held their reins. They bolted in a pack and Tate ran after them. Hero threw herself into me, and we both hit the ground seconds before a branch crashed into the place where I had been standing.

I expected a comment from her, but instead she just pulled me to my feet, and we started running after Tate and the horses. Another bolt of lightning hit a tree off to our left as we ran. More sparks shot out. The rain was slowing down, and the fire was growing. The flames licked at the trees, spreading and expanding as they chased us through the woods. I ran harder than I ever had in my life, with Hero racing along beside me, her dark hair billowing out behind her.

I saw the moment when the flames caught hold of her hair. I yelled. She whipped her head around to look at me, and her flaming hair swung with her. Hero's eyes widened, and a small sound escaped her mouth. But then she was throwing herself down and rolling back and forth in the mud. I took off my shoe and helped her beat out the last of the flames. And then she was up, and we were running again.

But the few seconds we had spent putting out one small fire had cost us our lead on the much larger blaze. Smoke was reaching for us, stretching to fill our lungs. I started having flashbacks of ogres and little girls as another shape came running toward us.

Tate let out a breath of relief when he saw us and then turned, falling into step beside us.

"You said you wanted a fire," Tate said.

Hero gave me an incredulous look. "You wanted a fire?" she panted.

"N-not like this."

Hero still didn't look sure of my sanity. She may have had a point.

Soon we came to a river. Tate had tied all three horses to a tree along the shore. The animals were panicking, Sparkles and Virtue with their bodies, Albert with his mouth.

I knew we didn't have much time.

"I didn't know where to go," Tate said.

"We'll have to c-cross the river," I told him.

Tate's face paled, and he shook his head.

"We h-have to," I told him. "The fire is c-coming."

Tate's face was terrified.

"He doesn't like rivers?" Hero said as she struggled to calm Virtue.

"H-he almost d-drowned in the last one," I said.

She looked at me seriously. "That seems like a fair reason not to like rivers."

It might have been fair, but it wasn't helpful. Putting the river between us and the fire was our best chance of surviving.

Lightning struck a third tree, and Albert reared. Screaming about the end being near, he pulled hard enough to snap the branch that held his reins. Albert took off galloping onto the river.

No, I do not mean into the river. The horse didn't plunge into the water. He ran over it, his hooves barely breaking the surface.

"There must be a sandbar," Hero cried and started untangling Virtue's reins from the tree.

Albert had either found solid land to use as a bridge, or Mildred the Wise had enchanted him with the ability to walk on water. I had to hope that she hadn't liked him that much.

"C-come on," I yelled to Tate.

The boy looked between the approaching fire and the running river. I grabbed his shoulders.

"You c-can do this."

Tate shook his head.

"You *n-need* to do this," I said and pushed him forward.

Tate took a tentative step into the river and then another.

I got Sparkles loose and then looked back at Hero. She had had to wrap her cloak around Virtue's head to get the horse to move, but they were following. On the far bank, I could see Albert running in spastic circles. He would live to panic another day.

Holding my breath and clutching Sparkles' reins, I stepped into the river. There was something under my foot. *Please be solid, please be solid,* I thought as I took another step. I was expecting rocks and a sudden drop but instead found a narrow strip of solid ground, the top of an old dam, maybe. The water was still moving and wanted to carry us off with it, but if we planted our feet firmly enough, we could stay on the submerged bridge.

Tate, Hero, the horses, and I all made it across the river and dropped down to sit in the mud. I had never been so happy to feel mud in my life.

From that side of the river, we watched the fire rush up and down the far bank, until finally another wave of heavy rain surged through and beat out the flames. The rain reached us, covering us in deluges of water, but no one minded. We had made it through, together.

When the rain finally stopped, we looked like a bunch of drowned rats. Hero pulled her hair over her shoulder and sighed at the sight of the blackened tips. She got up and went to dig into her saddle bags. She came back with a pair of scissors, which she held out to me.

"Will you cut my hair?"

"W-What?"

"Like a page boy?" Tate asked.

"Sh-she wouldn't look g-good with a pageboy."

"How else do you cut hair?" Tate said.

"Monks t-trim the t-top," I told him.

"True, but that would look even worse," he said.

"Just trim off the burned edges," Hero said in exasperation.

I still wasn't sure that I was the person who should be cutting a girl's hair, but I took the scissors. Hero sat down on a rock facing the river, and I walked around behind her. Only a few inches of her hair were black. If I did this right, her hair would still reach past the middle of her back, and no one would even notice.

I started on her left, trimming carefully. I made it almost to the middle before Tate gasped, and I turned.

"D-don't do that," I snapped at him.

"I saw a cardinal," he said happily. "They're good luck."

"We h-haven't had much g-good luck."

"Maybe now we will," he said.

And then we both looked back at Hero's hair. My stomach dropped a foot. Tate's eyes widened to the size of chicken eggs. When I'd turned in surprise, the scissors had slipped, cutting a diagonal wedge out of the middle of Hero's hair.

"H-how is this g-good luck," I whispered to Tate.

"It's in the back," Tate whispered.

"Everything all right?" Hero asked.

"Fine," Tate and I said together.

I quickly trimmed the black off the rest of her ends and said, "All d-done."

Hero pulled a length of hair over her shoulder, looked at the neatly trimmed ends, and then smiled up at me. "Thank you," she said.

I just nodded, fairly certain that hell hath no fury like a woman scalped. But maybe the cardinal had brought us good luck, because she didn't notice. And when Albert did and started to open his mouth, I shot him a look that threatened his very life. For once he kept his mouth shut.

The next day, we started climbing into the mountains. I was still worried about Hero somehow noticing her interesting hairstyle. I should have been worried about what was coming next.

CHAPTER 8
In Which We Are Set Upon by Bandits

We had little to eat other than turnips. I had come to despise that small, hard vegetable. Albert turned up his muzzle at them. Even Tate lost his cheerful expression when I pulled out the satchel. Hero was the only one who didn't seem to mind. But she hadn't been eating them nearly as long as the rest of us.

Late in the afternoon of our third day with Hero, we stopped to make camp. Once the horses were watered and the turnip soup was cooking over the fire, Hero said, "We have some time until supper is ready. How about a little sparring?"

"You mean with swords?" Tate asked.

"Of course," Hero said.

Tate and I looked at each other. From the look on his face, he had about as much experience with a sword as I did.

"W-well," I said, for once purposely dragging out a word, because I didn't know what to say next.

"It will be good for all of us," Hero said. "As Grand-father used to say, 'There is no substitute for practice.'"

Hero got *Guardian* out of my saddlebag and then went looking for a tree limb to serve as another blade. She gave me the sword, handed Tate the branch, and then stood back to watch.

Tate and I bowed to each other, because that seemed like the kind of thing that knights would do before they tried to cut off each other's heads. Then we began to swing our various weapons around. Hero's expression quickly shifted from patient expectation to confusion to revulsion.

She stepped closer and put a hand up to stop us. "What are you doing?"

Tate and I both looked slightly sheepish. I shrugged my shoulders.

"This is *Guardian*," Hero said. "You can't treat it like a stick. Don't you know anything about swordsmanship?"

I wanted to tell her that of course I did, but it would have been a lie. And she would have most likely asked to see some specific technique that I had no clue how to do. So I shook my head, feeling like an idiot.

"N-no," I said, and Tate nodded his agreement.

Hero frowned as she looked at me. I expected her to go on about what a disgrace I was, but instead she held out her hand. Feeling strange, I handed her the sword.

Hero walked around to face Tate. "First off, a sword is not a club that you swing. It should work like an extension of your arm." She moved her right arm through a series of movements to show us how natural the sword should look.

Hero taught us how to thrust and parry, how to slash and block. Tate and I took turns practicing the skills with *Guardian*. Hero's way certainly felt more effective. After that night, Hero gave Tate and me a swordsmanship lesson every evening while the stew cooked. Slowly, I began to feel less and less like a fool when I picked up *Guardian*.

The road was growing steeper and the air cooler. On occasion there would be a break in the trees, and we would get a real sense of how high we were climbing. The heights made Albert dizzy, and a wobbly horse is a danger to everyone. So we made a point of not letting him look. But one afternoon as we came around a tight turn, the forest disappeared to show a sheer drop ahead. Albert began to swoon.

I practically threw myself off his back and grabbed his reins.

"Everything's fine," I told him. "C-close your eyes."

Albert cried, "We are all going to fall to our deaths!"

"No, just c-close your eyes."

Albert begrudgingly closed his eyes.

"Now I'm g-going to lead you down the road.

His entire body was shaking. He moaned rather pitifully.

"C-come on now."

Albert slowly lifted one hoof and then another as I pulled the reins. He followed carefully after me. When we made it around the bend and into a small clearing, I told Albert that we were safe. He opened his eyes, looked at me, and fainted, knocking me to the ground in the process. I was trapped under an unconscious pile of horse, and it took both Tate and Hero to pull me out. Albert still didn't move. Sparkles rolled his eyes.

It was earlier in the day than we usually stopped, but we weren't going anywhere anytime soon, so Hero took out *Guardian* and started showing us how to hold a proper high guard. Our lesson came to a very abrupt end when two men came bursting through the trees. One carried a rusty sword, the other an old spear. Both figures were thin and filthy. Their clothes were torn. Their faces and arms were peppered with scars. They were two of the mean-est-looking men I had ever seen.

"Give us your gold, or we'll take the girl and run you both through," the man with the sword bellowed.

I glanced quickly around our group. Albert was thankfully still unconscious; this might have killed him. Tate stood in shock, with his hand gripped around the tree branch. Hero also stood still, but her eyes were narrowing.

"You will do no such thing," she said, and then lunged toward the man with the sword.

He stumbled back, wearing a look of shock, as Sir Danton's granddaughter came after him. In three strokes, she had knocked the rusty sword out of his hand and had the tip of *Guardian's* blade pressed against his throat.

The man's companion, staring openmouthed at his friend, didn't see Tate coming. Swinging his tree limb like a shepherd's staff, Tate knocked the spear-bearer to the ground.

"Hobart, get the lead rope," Hero said, without taking her eyes off the man who now knelt in front of her. He was easily twice her size but looked back at her in terror.

Still not quite believing what was happening, I untied the lead rope from Sparkle's harness and brought it back over to my friends. In minutes we had both bandits firmly tied.

"You two should be ashamed of yourselves," Hero said, once Tate's victim seemed able to look at her clearly. "Attacking children. Don't you have any sense of honor?"

The man who had come into the clearing brandishing a sword minutes before, began to wail.

Tate and I stared at each other. Hero continued to scowl at him.

"We never meant to be bandits!" the man cried. "We're respectable men."

"Respectable, my foot," Hero snapped.

"No, really," he said, as his friend tried to nod and ended up looking dizzy. "We were farmers until the crops failed. We never would have stooped to stealing if there were any other way to feed our families. Our whole village is starving."

Hero's expression softened, but her voice was still hard as she said, "Don't move."

Both men stared at the sword in her hand and nodded vigorously. Hero came over to confer with Tate and me.

"What do you think?" she asked in a whisper.

"They look awful hungry to me," Tate said.

I had to agree. Our would-be bandits looked like skin stretched over bone. I hated to think what the village's children must look like.

We turned back to the men.

"W-We'll take you back to your v-village," I told them. "If it's like you s-say, we'll let you go."

The men agreed, not that it mattered much, with Hero still holding *Guardian*. We revived Albert, introducing the strangers to him as fellow travelers. He must not have been in his right mind yet, because he didn't even comment about the fact that the men were bound with rope.

"That's a real interesting hairstyle," one of the men said to Hero as we started into the woods.

Tate and I both held our breath. But she just said, "It's the way all girls wear their hair at Castle Mortico."

The two men exchanged glances.

Three hours later, we reached their village. A crowd of people came out to meet us. Hero, Tate, and I just stared.

The people were like nothing I had ever seen before. Their cheeks were hollow, their arms and legs barely thicker than twigs. They looked at us with huge, hungry, hopeful eyes, as if maybe we could stop their suffering. Hero stared at a man and a woman who stood close together with a little girl tucked into the father's arms. Tate untied the bandits' ropes. I did the only thing I could think to do. I walked into the middle of the crowd and set down the magical bag of turnips. The people watched me, hesitant.

"It's a m-magic bag," I said. "No matter how many t-times you empty it, it will always f-fill up again with turnips."

A woman came cautiously forward and put her hand into the bag. She pulled out a turnip and bit into it. Her eyes lit up and she gobbled it down, reaching for another. The crowd started moving in. I knew the bag wasn't big enough for them to all reach into, so I turned it upside down. Turnips spilled out, pouring onto the ground. The villagers dove for them, eating and crying and talking all at once.

It was Tate who thought to hang the bag upside down from a tree, where it could continue to drop turnips. We stood back for a while, just watching. A festival was breaking out. As people reached their fill of turnips, they began to dance and sing, grasping handfuls of the small red vegetable in their upraised hands. There was music and singing. The children started to laugh.

We walked quietly away.

No one said much for the rest of the day. When night came, we built a fire, and Hero found us some wild onions to eat. After finishing our small meal, we sat just watching the flames.

"I've never seen people so h-hungry," I said.

"Or so happy," Hero added.

"It made me miss my family," Tate said.

Which made sense to me, having met Tate's relations.

"Do you miss your families?" Tate asked us.

"Some," I said honestly, and then looked over at Hero, expecting that anyone would be glad to be away from her family.

"I don't miss those people back at the castle," Hero said. "But I miss my mother and father and grandfather." Her eyes seemed far away, as if when she looked into the flames, she saw something very different from what Tate and I saw. "When I first came to live with Grandfather after my parents died, we would spend hours together in his library, reading and talking. I miss that. I miss him."

At her house, she was alone in a crowd of people. I guess we were alike in that way. We sat up half that night, telling stories about our lives growing up. In the morning, we passed into the province of Rona. We were nearly there.

CHAPTER 9
In Which We Reach the Castle

Hero and I might have been the only ones who could read the sign welcoming us into Rona, but everyone seemed to understand what it meant. We were less than a day's ride from the castle. Albert began to shake.

I reached down to pat his neck. "It's just a road. L-like any other."

Any road that leads to a dragon's lair.

Hero was clenching and unclenching her reins. Tate had started to whistle, a very high-pitched tune that grated against my ears. I didn't say anything to him about it. He had come all this way with me and would most likely be the one to take my body back to my family, if there was anything left.

The road dipped and turned and then passed through an archway of trees, the limbs reaching up to tangle with each other over our heads. It felt like we were riding through a rib cage. I couldn't see the sky, and that bothered me for some reason.

"Tate, why don't you tell us a s-story?" I said.

Tate frowned a little. "What kind of story?"

"Any k-kind," I said. Anything was better than the shrill whistling.

"All right."

Tate told us about a man who was sure that there was someone at the bottom of his well staring back at him. It was the kind of story that probably would have been funny under other circumstances, but on that morning, even Tate didn't enjoy it.

We found some berries and tried to eat at noon, but no one was really hungry. So we climbed back into our saddles and continued down the road. Less than an hour later, we came upon a man driving a flock of sheep.

"Excuse me, s-sir," I said. My voice seemed to tremble even more than usual. "W-we are looking for the dr-dragon who lives near h-here."

"He lives in the castle at the top of the mountain," the man said, pointing to the north.

I had kind of hoped that he would try to convince us to leave the creature alone, to run away and save ourselves, but he said nothing else. So we started down the road the stranger had pointed out.

The path wound around the mountain like a snake. There were no shrubs or trees. The entire mountainside was bare. As the castle grew closer, we could see that all of the outside walls had been blackened with fire.

I couldn't help but wonder how long it had taken the dragon to sear the building. Had it been a dozen breaths or just one? Had he burned the castle after he had conquered it or during the siege? What had happened to the people who had lived here? I wasn't certain that I wanted an answer to that last question.

No one spoke as we climbed, and I was thankful for the silence. What could any of us really say? Silence was better. Even Albert had stopped moaning. The wind that howled around us seemed to have taken over that duty.

Far too soon, we reached the end of the road and found ourselves facing two enormous gates. I slid off Albert's back and just stared. Tate and Hero came to stand with me.

"What do you suppose he has in there?" Tate whispered.

"Horses' bones," Albert moaned. "Hundreds and thousands of them."

"Maidens," Hero said quietly. "Girls he has stored away to eat later."

"I heard that dragons keep a token from each knight who comes to try and kill them. You know, something to remember each one," Tate said.

I wanted to tell them how unhelpful their comments were, but there wasn't any point in stammering out the words. I had thought every single thing they said.

Standing in front of that gate, I couldn't quite remember why I was there in the first place. It wasn't like I had a sister in there or something. I had just been looking for a noble deed, something to prove that I was worthy. There must be some other way to do that.

And even if there weren't, would it be so terrible to not earn a chance to go to the King's School for the Education of Future Knights? I could just go home and be pegged with rotting fruit for the rest of my life. There were worse things. At least I would be alive. And maybe I would have some enormous growth surge and suddenly become so tall and burly that no one would dare bother me. I knew it wasn't likely, but it was possible.

My friends wouldn't really mind if we turned back. Hero had at least had a break from her family. Tate had plenty of stories to share. And the way Albert would tell the tale, he would most likely come out as the bravest horse who ever lived.

Just when I had decided that the only sane thing to do was turn around and go home, I heard a scream—a long, anguished scream that made all of the hairs on my arms stand on end.

What kind of knight could hear that sound and walk away?

The scream faded, but it still echoed in my ears. I was fairly certain that it would haunt me for whatever was left of my brief life. I had to go.

"I'm going inside," I told them. Both Tate and Hero started to talk at once, but I interrupted, "I have to at least try to help her."

"I'm coming with you," Tate said, standing up a little taller as all of the color drained out of his face.

"No, you are going to make sure that everyone gets home," I said.

Hero opened her mouth, but I added, "And someone is going to need to finish teaching Tate how to use a sword."

They both looked like they were trying to come up with a new argument, but then another sound came from the castle. Not a scream this time, more a cry of despair.

"How will you get in?" Tate said.

"Through the gate."

Hero's eyes widened. "But then he'll know that you're here!"

"He already knows we're here," I said. "That's why the road winds around like that, so that the people in the castle can see who's coming. There's no break in the walls. We don't have any siege engines. If I'm going to get inside, it's going to be through that gate.

"Go a little way down the path," I told them. "If I'm not back in an hour, run."

"We are not going to leave you," Hero said, her chin rising up.

"If I'm not back in an hour, it means that I'm dead," I told her.

She still looked like she wanted to argue the point, but she eventually nodded. I guess she had to finally accept the truth of the situation.

I embraced Tate. "Give your family my thanks for everything.'"

He nodded, his blue eyes shining with tears.

I wasn't exactly sure what to do with Hero, but she threw her arms around me. "Be careful," she said.

I nodded as I drew back.

"We're real proud of you," Tate told me. The tears broke free now, streaming down his cheeks.

I waited while Tate and Hero got back into their saddles and then started down the road, Tate leading Albert behind him. And then I turned and walked toward the gate. My heart pounded out a warning, as if I didn't know that I was about to do something really stupid. Nausea threatened to empty my stomach at any moment. My legs had turned so wobbly that I couldn't seem to walk straight. But I still found myself at the gate long before I was ready to be there.

I lifted up one shaking fist and pounded on the wood. One. Two. Three times.

I stepped back, hoping that nothing would happen. But I never have been lucky. Slowly, the castle gate began to creak its way open.

CHAPTER 10
In Which I Come Nose-to-Nose with a Dragon

I braced myself, ready for the massive burst of flame that would roast me to a crisp. But instead of steam and smoke, I found a man dressed in livery. I wanted to tell him that I was there to rescue him and all the others, but my tongue lay dry and motionless in my mouth.

"Come in, young sir. Lord Rupert is expecting you," the man said.

Had another knight arrived before us? It really would be just my luck to come all this way only to have someone else take on the monster before I could. Or was this Lord Rupert being held captive? Or maybe he didn't even exist. Maybe this was all some sort of trap. I wanted to confer with Hero and Tate, but if I went back down the road to where they were waiting, I would only draw attention to them.

The man stepped back and gestured for me to follow. I walked slowly through the gateway and into a garden complete with neat paths, banks of flowers, and a fountain in the center shaped like a dragon. The last owners had all but sent the beast an invitation.

We passed through the garden and came to a huge pair of golden doors engraved with the sun, moon, and stars. My guide opened the doors, and we walked into a massive hall, wide enough for a dozen horsemen to ride abreast. The ceiling soared above us.

I kept waiting for the attack, for the floor to begin vibrating under an enormous weight, or for a roar to shake the tapestries that lined the walls. But all I heard was the echo of our footsteps. The waiting was its own cruel torture.

Then the liveried man stopped beside a set of intricately carved doors. Somehow, I knew that the dragon was on the other side of those doors. What I didn't understand was why this balding man was so willingly bringing me to it. Maybe the beast had his family held captive.

The servant opened the doors and stepped back.

With a heart rate that would have been well suited to escaping a wildfire, I walked into a space like nothing I had ever seen before. It was a round room, larger than the Great Hall at Castle Mortico. The walls were covered in shelves filled with enormous leatherbound books and dozens of brass instruments. A glass dome took the place of a ceiling. In the center of the room stood a large table, and beside it, the dragon.

The beast was bigger than I had imagined. His hide was ruby red. His wings were folded against his back, but I could picture how wide they must be if they were able to lift the creature off the ground. The dragon was looking away from us, but if what I had heard of dragons was true, he could most certainly smell us.

"My lord, the young gentleman has arrived," my escort announced.

"Oh, good," said a deep, rumbling voice, and then the massive head began to turn.

I knew that I should draw *Guardian*, but my arms refused to move. It was as if my limbs had been forged out of iron.

The dragon's head swung slowly around to face us, and I found myself staring into dark eyes that looked back at me through enormous spectacles balanced on the end of its snout.

"Welcome, young sir. I am so glad that you arrived in time," the dragon said in his deep voice. "I had despaired that Hopkins and I would be viewing alone this year."

I just stood staring at the beast.

"What is your name, if I may ask?" the dragon continued in what I could only call a pleasant tone.

My voice sounded hollow as I said the words, "Hobart of Finnagen."

"Ah, Finnagen, a lovely village," the dragon said. "I visited there some three hundred years ago. Though I suppose all of the fine people I met there have passed." His face became rather thoughtful, but then he shook his great head. "Listen to me, reminiscing, when we have not even been properly introduced. I am, of course, Lord Rupert of Flamegon, and this is my assistant, Hopkins."

Hopkins bowed slightly to me. Lord Rupert held out a great claw. I had no idea what to do. My understanding of manners did not extend to this situation. But I did at least know that it was not wise to insult a dragon, so I walked forward. Hoping he wouldn't notice how badly my hands were sweating, I took hold of one talon. Lord Rupert lifted my feet off the floor and then set me down again, and I supposed that we had officially shaken hands. I knew that I was shaken.

I stepped back, still trying to decide what to think of this enormous creature, when Lord Rupert suddenly jumped, clasped his front claws to his jaw, and screamed. It was the same high-pitched sound we had heard from outside the castle.

Hopkins snatched up a broom and came running forward. He lifted it high, and I quickly drew *Guardian*. But he didn't swing the broom at me. Instead, Hopkins brought it down to the floor with a crash, lifted it again, and continued running and swinging. As he dodged around the large table, I could see that he was chasing a spider about the size of my thumb. The spider ran up a wall, out of Hopkins' reach, and then scrambled over to the seam where the glass-domed roof began.

"We will catch him next time, my lord," Hopkins said, slightly out of breath.

Rupert nodded and then glanced over at me with obvious embarrassment. "I do not care for spiders," he said.

"Neither does my horse," I heard myself saying.

"Oh, yes, your companions!" Lord Rupert said. "Here you have been so kind to come in advance in order to present them, and I become distracted by a stray arachnid. Please, tell me about your friends. Are they experienced astronomers?"

"Not that they've ever mentioned," I said slowly.

"Not to worry," Lord Rupert said. "The Flamegon Comet is a wondrous sight for both novice and scholar alike. But we should hurry. I would love to share a meal together before it grows dark enough for our viewing. Would you like Hopkins to go down to retrieve your companions?"

"No, I should go myself," I said.

"Of course."

I walked out of the castle and down the road to either invite my friends to dinner or suggest that we flee. I still wasn't sure which would be the wiser choice. I had barely made it around the first bend, when Hero suddenly appeared and threw her arms around me.

"We were so worried," she told me. "Is it dead? Were there any other survivors?"

"I didn't kill the dragon."

Tate put a hand on my shoulder. "Well, that's all right. You went in and faced one. How many people can say that?"

"This isn't your typical dragon," I said carefully.

Both of them looked at me with confused expressions.

"It's small?" Hero asked.

"No, he's enormous."

"It has no fangs or claws?" Tate said.

"No, he has both in good supply."

"What, then?" Hero's voice was growing insistent.

"He's—" I paused, trying to come up with the right word. "He's a gentleman."

Tate and Hero stared at me in disbelief. So I told them everything that had happened since I left them. Hero was concerned that it might be a trap. Tate was eager to catch a glimpse of Lord Rupert of Flamegon and pointed out that I still needed to kill the beast if I wanted to get into knight school.

"We can be witnesses," Tate told her.

Hero was still reluctant, and we had to blindfold Albert, but we all went back to the castle together. Hopkins met us at the gate and escorted the three horses into the stable before leading us back to the observatory.

Once again, Lord Rupert could not have been more gracious.

"Lady Hero, it is my great honor to make your acquaintance," he said in the midst of a deep bow. "Master Tate, I welcome you to Castle Flamegon. It is a pleasure to have you join us for the viewing tonight."

Soon Hero, Tate, and I were all seated at a large dining table in the castle's Great Hall. Like the other rooms we would encounter on the first floor, it was built to dragon proportions. Lord Rupert did not require a chair but oversaw the meal from the head of the table.

"I discovered the comet four hundred and twenty-eight years ago, when I was little more than a hatchling," Lord Rupert told us after our main course of vegetable stew had been cleared away. (Lord Rupert was a vegetarian.) "It was the year before my cousin Harold decided to scorch the sides of the castle for effect. He thought that a castle called Flamegon should look singed. He never did have much of an eye for aesthetics."

Lord Rupert's dark eyes grew deep and heavy. "Harold is gone now. They all are." He looked over at us, seeming almost pained by the sight. "Ah, when we are young, we think we are immortal, but the years will pass, and you will bury those you love. Whether your life is destined to last fifty years or five hundred, I promise you that it will pass too quickly."

Hopkins stepped into the doorway and nodded to his lord.

"But now is not the time for the thoughts of a lonely old soul. It is time for the event that brings us all together. Come, come. We do not want to miss it, for the comet will not pass this way again for another one hundred and seven years."

We followed Lord Rupert's swinging tail back across the hall toward the observatory. Even I could tell that each step pained him.

"What's your plan?" Tate asked me in a hushed tone.

"I don't know." The thought of drawing a sword on this ancient creature seemed—wrong.

We gathered under Lord Rupert's glass dome and watched his comet streak across the sky. Hero gasped at the sight of it, and Tate stood slack jawed. It really was that astounding. When the spectacle had passed and our mugs of hot chocolate were empty, Hopkins showed us to our rooms.

On the second floor of Castle Flamegon—which was thankfully built for human guests—I stretched out on the feather mattress and stared up at the underside of my canopied bed. As I had traveled up the mountain, all I could think about was how could *I* kill this dragon? Now all I could think was how could I kill *this* dragon?

Lord Rupert was not a beast who terrorized the surrounding countryside, stealing treasures and eating maidens. He was a kind old gentleman scholar. How could I possibly take the life of this gentle giant?

The answer pressed down on my chest like a boulder. I couldn't. And there was no time left to find a fouler creature. It was already April. May Day would come. I would have no great deed to speak for me and no chance of being allowed to take the entrance exam.

My dreams of becoming a knight had died the moment I decided to spare Lord Rupert's life.

CHAPTER 11
In Which I Travel Home Again

Lord Rupert and my friends were in a fine mood when I came down the next morning. Hero was entranced by the dragon's collection of books. Lord Rupert was thoroughly enjoying one of Tate's stories, and Tate seemed thrilled with his rapt audience.

Hero looked up and saw me as I came into the library. She closed her book and walked back to where I stood just inside the doorway.

"What did you decide to do?" she whispered.

"I can't hurt him."

Hero nodded. She glanced over at Lord Rupert and then back at me. "Have you noticed that you lost your stutter?"

I stared at her as I thought back over my words of the past day. She was right. My stutter was gone; but even that didn't make me feel any better.

Hopkins called us to breakfast, and we all walked back across the hall to the dining room. Distracted, I didn't notice Lord Rupert's tail inadvertently swinging my way until it had splattered me against a wall. I had to peel myself off the stone before I could go in and find my chair. The table was heaped with griddle cakes and tureens of maple syrup. The pile of food in front of Lord Rupert was the size of a large boulder.

When the meal had ended, a massive tear came into one of the dragon's dark eyes. "I suppose you will be going," he said, looking slightly pained.

Tate nodded. "Our families will be worrying about us."

Lord Rupert nodded his great head. "I do understand; but I dare hope that you might come to visit me again. You could stay as long as you wished."

Hero patted one massive claw. "We'll come back."

"Perhaps for the summer solstice," Lord Rupert said with a hopeful expression.

Tate nodded.

"Maybe so," was the best I could promise.

Lord Rupert walked us out as far as the garden courtyard. Hopkins brought out the horses, groomed and saddled. Our saddlebags were once again full and smelled of fresh provisions and warm chocolate chip cookies.

"Safe travels," Lord Rupert called to us and then pulled out an enormous handkerchief to dab at his eyes.

"Thank you for everything," Tate called back.

And we left Castle Flamegon.

Albert talked for the majority of the trip down the mountain. He told us all about his stay and the quality of the oats. We were nearly at the base before he seemed to remember that we had gone there so that I could kill something.

"That dragon seemed very much alive when we left," Albert said.

I didn't comment.

"He wasn't anything like the dragons from the stories," Hero told my horse. "It would have been dishonorable to kill him."

She said that as if I had any honor to consider.

Tate glanced from Hero to me. "Maybe you'll have better luck next year."

"I'll be too old next year," I mumbled.

Hero whispered something to Tate, but their pity couldn't change anything. Unless I wanted to become a bandit or the world's worst minstrel, I was doomed to a life of being pegged with rotting fruit.

When we came out of the mountains of Rona, we reached a fork in the road. Hero pointed to the westward branch. "This road will take you straight home."

I didn't really want to go home, but I couldn't think of a good reason why I should take the longer route, so we said goodbye. They were my first real friends. It was hard to see them go.

Albert and I traveled on alone. The same trip that had seemed to take months of travel on the way to Rona passed by in just over a week by this more direct route. And the day soon came when we reached the village of Gretten. I paused outside Mildred's door. She was the first person who had taken my quest seriously, and now I had to tell her that I had failed. I stood there, staring at the wooden door, unable to bring myself to knock. Finally, I turned and went back to climb into my saddle.

"We aren't going to visit Mildred?" Albert asked as I turned him away from the cottage.

"No."

Albert sighed. "I wanted to tell her all about our adventures. She loves my stories."

I didn't comment.

I was in no hurry to get home, and what had taken me a day on foot at the beginning of my journey took me nearly as long on horseback. But eventually, Albert and I reached the village of Finnagen, a little after sundown.

The streets were quiet but not yet fully dark. Without scores of mockers yelling insults at me, I looked around, maybe for the first time, and saw that Lord Rupert was right. Finnagen really was a nice little village. And in a strange way, I was glad to be home. At least, I figured I would be glad to be home until my first run-in with William.

I led Albert through the sea of pigpens, ignoring his complaints about the smell, and got him settled in the barn before walking up to the house. Again, I paused in front of a door. But this door flew open. My mother stared at me for two breaths and then began to cry. Wrapping her arms around me, she pulled me into the house. Then everyone started talking at once. My brothers were asking where I had been and telling me how far they had gone looking for me. My mother cried into my neck, telling me how worried she had been. My father said that he was going to tan my hide. I just stood there, not having any idea what to do.

It had never occurred to me that they would worry about me or even miss me while I was gone. They had forgotten me so many times that I thought they wouldn't even notice. But from what I could make out through the tangle of voices, they had really worried.

Maude came in with the food, set down the dishes, and came over to wrap her arms around me. "'Tis good to have you home," she said into my hair.

Then we ate, my mother urging food into me until I thought I might burst. My brothers were in awe of *Guardian* and wanted to know how I had come by a legendary blade. And after supper, they insisted on meeting Albert, who told them all about our adventures. His tale was only loosely connected to fact, but my family enjoyed hearing it almost as much as Albert enjoyed telling it.

The next day, I woke up sore and happy, until my brother George told me that we had to leave for the May Day festival.

All the way to King's City, I hoped that the nominations would be cancelled for some reason. But of course, they weren't. And I had to stand in the crowd and watch as boy after boy was presented, each with a list of noble deeds. William of Finnagen was the first. He shot me a nasty grin as he climbed the steps onto the stage and took his place in front of the crowd.

The Lord of Finnagen had always brought in the best tutors for his nephew. So I had assumed that William would be staying at home to study to be a knight. He didn't need a free education. But perhaps he liked the idea of training with the king's own sons.

"Wasn't this knight school why you set out on your quest in the first place?" Albert asked me.

I grumbled something.

"Why doesn't someone nominate you?" he said.

"Because you can't be nominated by your own family," I said. "And at the moment, they are the only people who think I'm worthy."

"I think you're worthy," Albert said.

"You're a horse."

"I don't see why that should matter."

"And you're biased. You just want to get to be a knight's steed."

"True," he said.

The king granted twenty-seven boys the opportunity to take the entrance exam for knight school before he said, "Are there any further nominations?"

The people crowded into the square looked around at each other, but not a single person raised a hand.

"Very well," the king said. He took a deep breath in preparation for his annual commissioning speech, and then paused. A dark shape was moving overhead.

The king looked up, and the crowd followed his eyes. There were more than a few screams as the people realized what was coming toward them. I saw the dragon's great shape, and for an instant, I thought that this could be my chance. If I killed this beast in front of the crowd, surely three people would be willing to nominate me. I placed a hand on *Guardian's* hilt, ready to take one last chance at greatness, and then I dropped my hand again.

It was a very familiar dragon who landed on the platform with a thud and folded his great wings. The great dragon turned his large head, taking in the crowd through his spectacles, before turning to the king with a bow.

"Your Majesty," he said in his deep voice. "I am Lord Rupert of Flamegon, who once served your noble grandfather. I would like to nominate one more candidate for your fine school."

It has been my experience that most people are more than happy to go along with whatever a dragon says. The king was no exception. He nodded, looking rather pale, as he stared at Lord Rupert's teeth.

"I would like to nominate Hobart of Finnagen, who showed his worthiness by taking the time to visit a lonely old creature."

I stared at Lord Rupert, not really certain what to say. Before I could collect my words, Tate and Hero came bursting onto the platform. They were both breathless and excited. Behind them came a great collection of people.

Tate spoke in a loud, clear voice. "On two separate occasions, Hobart of Finnagen saved my life, at risk of his own."

"He built us a bridge that we sorely needed," Dan the Slight added.

"He gave me the courage to overcome my fear of the sea," the fisherman said.

And then a dozen individuals, bedecked in turnip jewelry, stepped forward. "He saved our village from starvation by giving us the last food he had," one of their number called out.

Hero was watching me when she said, "He offered me friendship when I greatly needed it."

The king looked from Hero to the crowd. "Where is young Hobart of Finnagen?" he asked.

"Here," my brother Robert called out, pointing at me.

"Come forward, young man," the king said.

The crowd opened a path for me, and I walked shakily forward. My face felt as if I had been leaning into a fire. I couldn't believe this was happening. But then my feet were carrying me up the steps and onto the platform. I took a knee, bowing my head before my king. When I looked up, he was gazing out at the crowd.

"We often hear about fantastic feats performed by knights," he said. "But may we never forget that a knight is first and foremost a servant sworn by the oath of chivalry to care for and protect those in need." The king looked down at me. His expression was serious, but his eyes seemed pleased. "I therefore deem that Hobart of Finnagen is more than worthy to take the entrance examination."

I knelt there in shock as the people began to cheer. My nominators chanted my name, and the crowd soon joined them. I did finally find my voice long enough to thank the king, a moment before Tate and Hero threw themselves at me. I hugged them both but had to settle for wrapping my arms around Lord Rupert's claw.

The next day, I took the entrance exam. I never have been lucky, but it turns out that effort is even more useful. I was determined, and my experiences of the past few weeks helped immensely. I could climb and balance, ride a horse, and run as well as any of the others. And thanks to Hero's instruction, I could even hold my own with a sword. I passed the test.

And so, Tate set out for Fair Oaks with yet another story to tell. Hero went to live with Lord Rupert, where they studied and read together in happy companionship. My family went home again. And I entered the King's School for the Education of Future Knights.

You might wonder what happened there. But that is another story altogether.

THE END

If you enjoyed this book, please take a few minutes and write a review on Amazon or Goodreads. I would greatly appreciate it!

And be sure to visit me at www.heathermullaly.com.

Acknowledgements

When I was nine years old, my uncle gave me a copy of *Ramona Forever,* by Beverly Cleary. He inscribed the book:
To Heather, just for being Heather
Love, Uncle Butch
It was a gift I treasured, and still have, in large part because of the inscription. And it was that copy of *Ramona Forever* that I was reading to my daughter when I first got the idea for *The Legend of Hobart.*

Thank you to the members of my family for cultivating my love of books through good stories, inscribed hardbacks, and time curled up on the couch reading together. I love to write because I love to read. And I love to read because of all of you.

Thank you to all of the kids who served as fearless beta readers for this book. And to Hannah for drawing the first illustration of Sir Rupert of Flamegon.

Thanks to Julia Tomiak, Carey Evans, and Richael Ighodalo for your thoughts and ideas. And to Lara Kennedy for your editing prowess.

And as always, to Tom and our girls, thank you for your love and encouragement through this bumpy journey we call life.

1 Peter 4:10

9 781736 477373